Tommy's New Bed

by Pnina Moed-Kass
illustrated by Turi MacCombie

A GOLDEN BOOK • NEW YORK
Western Publishing Company, Inc.
Racine, Wisconsin 53404

Tommy's Daddy is moving Tommy's crib out of the bedroom into the hall.

"This crib is too little for you. But it's just right for your new cousin," says Daddy.

The doorbell rings.
It's a delivery—a big box.
"My new bed! My new bed!"
Tommy cries.

Tommy helps Mommy and Daddy put the
new bed together.

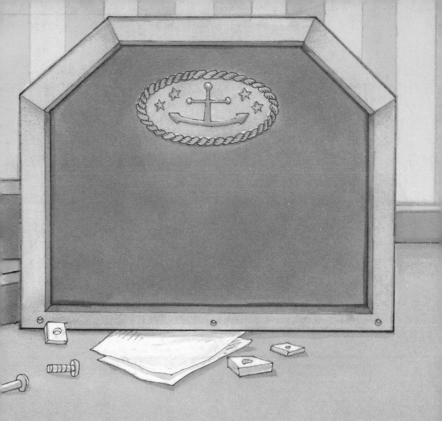

The bed is made of shiny brown wood. On the headboard are an anchor and four stars.

It looks like a ship captain's bed. And it is very grown-up. It has no sides.

Tommy jumps up and down on the mattress
until Mommy tells him to stop.

There are new sheets for the bed. On the sheets are sailboats and sailors in red, white, and blue.

On the pillowcase are waves and sails. The
blanket is ocean blue.

Tommy puts his favorite things on the bed.
He puts Curtis the pop-up clown under the
anchor. He puts Teddy on the pillow.
There is still plenty of room for Tommy.

That night Tommy eats quickly.

He rushes to take a bath.

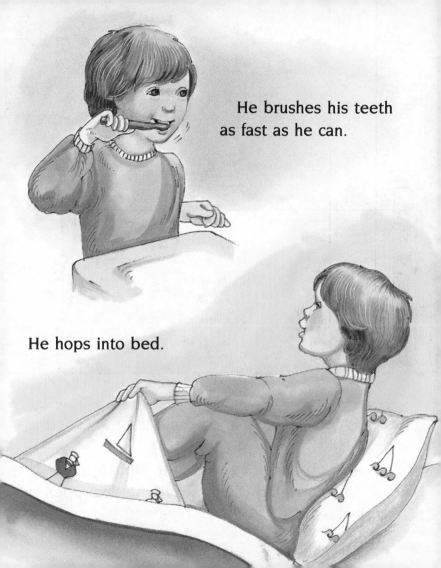

He brushes his teeth
as fast as he can.

He hops into bed.

Mommy and Daddy come in to say good night.

"Sleep tight, Captain," says Mommy.

Mommy and Daddy leave the door open just a crack.

Tommy stretches out his legs. He stretches out his arms.

Then he curls up near the edge
of the bed and goes to sleep.

Suddenly Tommy wakes up. He is on the floor in the dark. He has fallen out of his new bed.

Tommy rubs his head. The new bed isn't nice after all!

Tommy goes into the hall
There is his old crib.

He climbs in. He puts Teddy in the corner.
He lies close to the sides. He goes to sleep.

In the morning Tommy wakes up. His daddy is there. Daddy says, "Hi, Tommy. It looks like you took a trip last night.

Tonight we'll tuck you very tightly in your new bed and you won't fall out."

After supper Tommy climbs into his new
bed. He lies in the very middle. Teddy lies
next to him.

Mommy and Daddy tuck Tommy and Teddy
in extra tight.

"Where are you sailing tonight?" asks Daddy.

"I'm staying right here!" says Tommy.

And he does.